Pigs

A Level Two Reader

By Cynthia Klingel and Robert B. Noyed

The
Child's
World®

2

"Oink." "Snort." "Squeal."
What animals make
these sounds? Pigs make
these sounds!

Most pigs live on farms. Pigs have thick bodies. Some people might call them fat.

4

A pig's skin is thick and covered with hair. Pigs like to roll in the mud to cool off.

Pigs have a round nose called a snout. They also have a short curly tail. Pigs have four short legs.

A male pig is called a boar.

A female pig is called a sow.

Baby pigs are called piglets. A sow can have eight to twelve piglets at a time. Piglets drink their mother's milk and grow very fast.

On farms, pigs eat corn, oats, and other grains. Pigs will eat almost anything.

Most pigs are raised for meat. This meat is called pork. Pigs are also raised for their skin.

Pigskin is made into leather. Many footballs are made from pigskin. Belts, wallets, and gloves are also made from pigskin.

Pigs are smart animals. They can learn tricks. Some people have pigs as pets. Would you like a pig as a pet?

Index

To Find Out More

Books

Gibbons, Gail. *Pigs.* New York: Holiday House, 1999.

King-Smith, Dick, and Anita Jeram (illustrator). *All Pigs Are Beautiful.* Cambridge, Mass.: Candlewick Press, 1993.

Murray, Peter. *Pigs.* Chanhassen, Minn.: The Child's World, 1998.

Wolfman, Judy, and David Lorenz Winston (photographer). *Life on a Pig Farm.* Minneapolis: Carolrhoda Books, 1998.

Web Sites

Breeds of Livestock: Swine
http://www.ansi.okstate.edu/breeds/swine/
Information about all breeds of pigs.

Note to Parents and Educators

Welcome to The Wonders of Reading™! These books provide text at three different levels for beginning readers to practice and strengthen their reading skills. Additionally, the use of nonfiction text provides readers the valuable opportunity to *read to learn*, not just to learn to read.

These leveled readers allow children to choose books at their level of reading confidence and performance. Level One books offer beginning readers simple language, word choice, and sentence structure as well as a word list. Level Two books feature slightly more difficult vocabulary, longer sentences, and longer total text. In the back of each Level Two book are an index and a list of books and Web sites for finding out more information. Level Three books continue to extend word choice and length of text. In the back of each Level Three book are a glossary, an index, and a list of books and Web sites for further research.

State and national standards in reading and language arts emphasize using nonfiction at all levels of reading development. The Wonders of Reading™ fill the historical void in nonfiction material for the primary grade readers with the additional benefit of a leveled text.

About the Authors

Cindy Klingel has worked as a high school English teacher and an elementary teacher. She is currently the curriculum director for a Minnesota school district. Writing children's books is another way for her to continue her passion for sharing the written word with children. Cindy Klingel is a frequent visitor to the children's section of bookstores and enjoys spending time with her many friends, family, and two daughters.

Bob Noyed started his career as a newspaper reporter. Since then, he has worked in communications and public relations for more than fourteen years for a Minnesota school district. He enjoys writing books for children and finds that it brings a different feeling of challenge and accomplishment from other writing projects. He is an avid reader who also enjoys music, theater, traveling, and spending time with his wife, son, and daughter.

Published by The Child's World®, Inc.
PO Box 326
Chanhassen, MN 55317-0326
800-599-READ
www.childsworld.com

Photo Credits
© Andy Sacks/Tony Stone Images: 21
© Andy Sacks/Tony Stone Worldwide: 9
© Ben Osborne/Tony Stone Worldwide: 10
© Flanagan Publishing Services/Romie Flanagan: 17, 18
© Gary John Norman/Tony Stone Images: cover
© Gay Bumgarner/Tony Stone Worldwide: 6
© James L. Digby/Photri, Inc.: 14
© Peter Cade/Tony Stone Images: 5
© Photri, Inc.: 13
© 1991 Sharon Cummings/Dembinsky Photo Assoc. Inc.: 2

Project Coordination: Editorial Directions, Inc.
Photo Research: Alice K. Flanagan

Library of Congress Cataloging-in-Publication Data
Klingel, Cynthia Fitterer.
Pigs / by Cynthia Klingel and Robert B. Noyed.
p.   cm. — (Wonder books)
Summary: A simple introduction to the physical characteristics and behavior of pigs.
ISBN 1-56766-822-4 (alk. paper)
1. Swine—Juvenile literature.   [1. Pigs.]
I. Noyed, Robert B.   II. Title.   III. Wonder books (Chanhassen, Minn.)

SF395.5 .K65   2000
636.4—dc21   99-057537